This is one of a series of books specially prepared for very young children.

The simple text tells the story of each picture and the bright, colourful illustrations will promote lively discussion between child and adult.

Published by Ladybird Books Ltd Loughborough Leicestershire UK
Ladybird Books Inc Auburn Maine 04210 USA

Printed in England (3)

Ladybird Toddler Books

on
the farm

written by MARY HURT

illustrated by PAT OAKLEY
HURLSTON DESIGN

Ladybird Books

It is a sunny day on the farm.
The farmer is very busy.
There are lots of new baby animals.

Here is the farmer on his tractor.
He gets up very early each morning.
Here he is planting seeds.
He hopes that they will grow into
strong plants.

This is the farmer's house.
It is a big house.
Around the house is the farm-yard.
Can you see where the farmer
keeps his tractor?

The hens live here.
They lay big brown eggs each day.
The farmer's wife collects them
in a basket.

Some baby chicks are here.
They are soft and fluffy.
They will stay by the mother hen.
She will keep them warm
with her soft feathers.

Who is this handsome bird?
He sings a very loud song.
Cock-a-doodle-do!

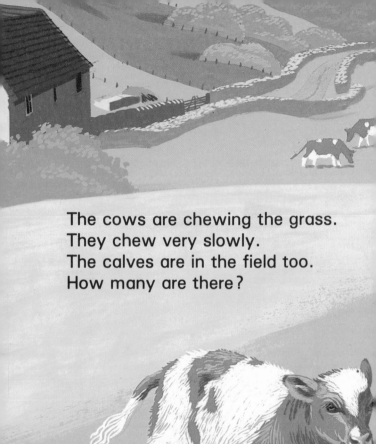

The cows are chewing the grass.
They chew very slowly.
The calves are in the field too.
How many are there?

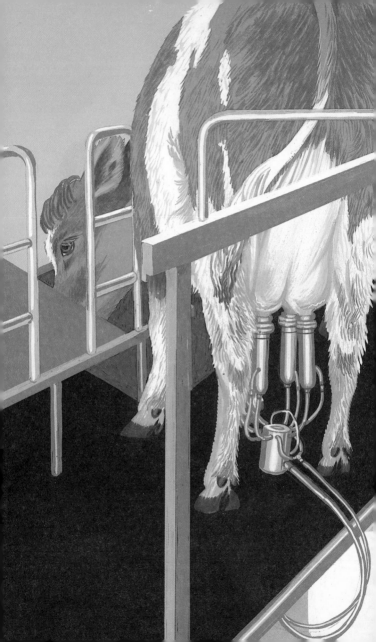

The cows are being milked here.
The machine sucks milk from the cows.
They have some food while they are
being milked.
When milking is over, the machine is
taken off the cow.

Here is the milk-tanker.
It will collect the milk and take it
to the dairy.

The farmer has some horses and a foal.
They sleep here in the stable.
In the day-time they gallop in the field.
The children from the farm ride
on the horses.

Here is the combine harvester.
It is a very big machine.
It cuts the wheat for the farmer.

Straw has been put into bales.
They are being lifted on to the trailer.
The farmer will keep the straw
in the barn.

Here is the barn.
The farm cat lives here.
She has made a soft bed for her
new kittens.

The sheep are here.
Some are eating the grass.
The lambs are playing.
They skip and run in the field.

Here is the farm dog helping the farmer.
The farmer whistles to tell the dog
what to do.
The dog will run round the sheep and
help to get them through the gate.

The pigs live here in the pig sty.
They need a lot of food to make them
grow strong.
Look at their curly tails.

These goats live on the farm.
They also give milk to the farmer.
Have you tasted goat's milk?

The ducks are here
with five baby ducklings.
They are quacking loudly.
They are hungry.

What is growing on this farm?
Can you see wheat, potatoes and
cabbages?
They need sunshine and rain to make
them grow.
Then the farmer will sell them.

Some of the animals are here
with the farmer.
Brown calves, a woolly sheep, a hen,
some chicks, a goat and three little
kittens.
Say goodbye to them!